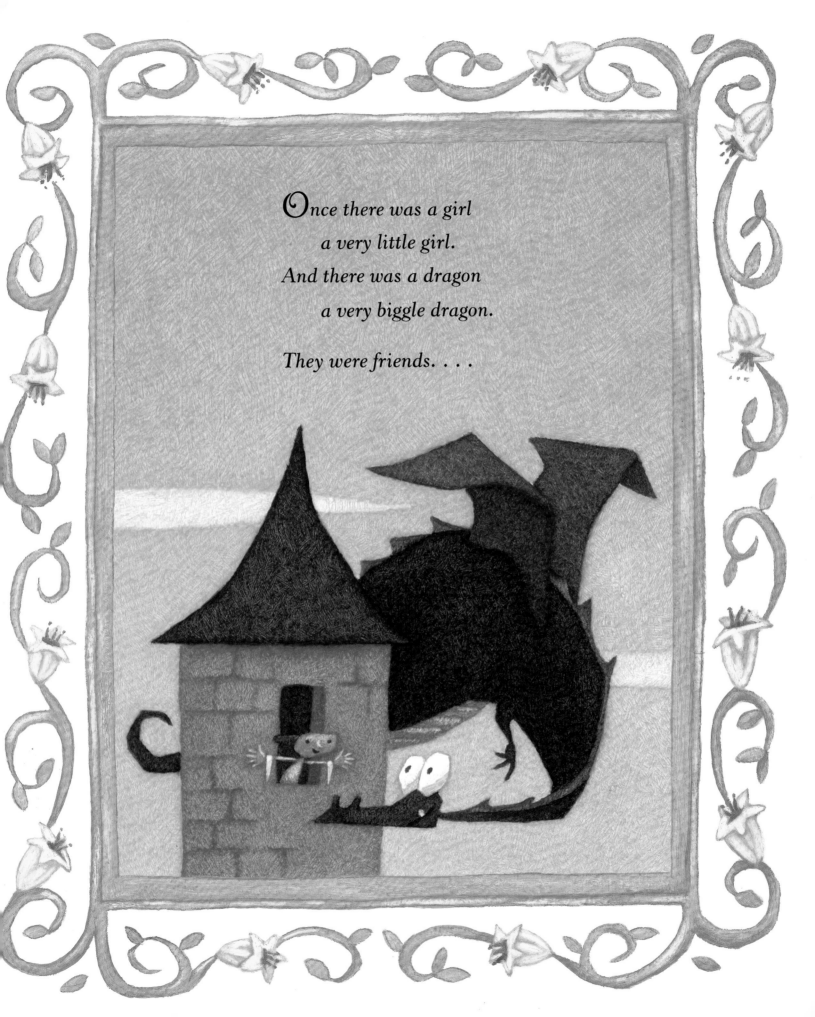

Once there was a girl
a very little girl.
And there was a dragon
a very biggle dragon.

They were friends. . . .

Evermore Dragon

Barbara Joosse

illustrated by Randy Cecil

Candlewick Press

$\mathcal{A}$t the wake of derry-day

the friends decided what to play.

Hide-and-seek? Hide-and-seek!

Okay, okay.

Dragon jumped up and down,

made a rum-below sound.

"Goodie, goodie, goodie!

Me first!"

Girl closed her eyes

so Dragon could hide.

Dragon found a little rock

such a very little rock

and he curled his Dragon self

his Drag-enormo self

into a dragon ball,

which wasn't—no, it wasn't—small at all!

Girl opened her eyes.

There was Dragon, yo ho.

But she climbed up a tree.

"Oh, where can Dragon be?"

And she peeked inside his lair.

"No, he isn't there."

And she stood upon a rock

such a very little rock

and she sighed a little sigh

such a very little sigh. Oh, my.

"Dragon's *so* good at hiding,

I'm not sure I can find him.

What to do?"

"BOO!"

Girl wrapped her arms around him

so everly around him.

"Oh, Dragon, you're so clever.

You're the smartest dragon ever."

And he knew

it was true.

"Now you!"

Girl ran

and ran

and ran . . .

to a faraway place

   such a hidey-hole place

and she didn't make a sound

   not a single little sound . . .

shhhhh.

And she waited for Dragon

so long for Dragon

to be found by Dragon

and she stretched and she yawned and

ZZZZZZZZZ.

Dragon looked everywhere—every here, every there—

in the leaves

of the trees . . .

from the log

in the bog . . .

off the ridge of the bridge . . .

No Girl.

"Girl?" bellowed Dragon.
"Are you lost?" bellowed Dragon.

And she was.

Girl woke, and it was night.

Deep deep dark night.

No stars. No moon.

No castle. No room.

No best friends together.

Just Girl.

Came the cricking and the cracking,

came the flipping and the flapping,

came the moaning and the groaning—

are there monsters in the night?

Oh, she tried so not to cry!

But she cried silver tears

worry worry tears

and her heart thumped a sound

a trem-below sound

that only Dragon friends,

very *very* special friends, can hear.

"Girl!" thundered Dragon.
"I hear you!" thundered Dragon.

And he breathed his dragon fire

and it lit up the sky

made a bright night sky

and he flew through the night

All right!

"Girl!" roared Dragon.

"I am here!" roared Dragon.

AND HE WAS!

Dragon wrapped his wings around her

so everly around her.

"I am here," rumbled Dragon.

"You're a dear," whispered Girl.

Dragon held her and he sang,
"Evermore, evermore, I am here."

And she knew

it was true.

For Esme, who is
a little bit Dragon and a little bit Girl
B. J.

For Strummer, Clint, and Jude
R. C.

First edition 2015

Library of Congress Catalog Card Number 2014950529
ISBN 978-0-7636-6882-2

15 16 17 18 19 20 CCP 10 9 8 7 6 5 4 3 2 1

Printed in Shenzhen, Guangdong, China

This book was typeset in Horley Old Style Semibold.
The illustrations were done in oil.

Candlewick Press
99 Dover Street
Somerville, Massachusetts 02144

visit us at www.candlewick.com